MOVING THROUGH
TIME

MOVING THROUGH
TIME

STEVE BENIDITO

Print information available on the last page.

Rev. date: 01/14/2019

To order additional copies of this book, contact:
Xlibris
1-888-795-4274
www.Xlibris.com
Orders@Xlibris.com
544111

ACKNOWLEDGMENTS

I am indebted to the following people for their help and support:

I would like to thank my family for their prayers and support. Thanks Mom. Love you Dad.

To my brother, Calvin, I miss you. Your love reminds me to never take life for granted, and to cherish every moment and I will.

To Tyrone. Thanks for everything, and I do mean everything. Period.

To all my true friends. You know who you are. Thanks for pushing and encouraging me all the time. What a group of friends.

Miss you, West. Tears still flow.

Special thanks to Mariatotino Mariachristina for your input.

Grazie Ancora.

To my publishing team. Thanks for all your professionalism and dedication. I tip my hat off to you all.

Bello Bello

CHAPTER ONE

It was a nice, hot comfortable summer's day, in the 80's on the streets of Queens. Life was good, whether you was a bum or a drug dealer. As a youth everyone was trying to find themselves. Many was using their God given talent like that show fame. One afternoon on the street a couple of boys are break dancing on ther corner, which draws a crowd. A member of a local Spanish gang is standing on the side called the seven mordes.

"Come on fellas, lets go" said one Member.
Approaching the crowd with the idea of making money by collecting it from the crowd for watching the two boys break dance.
Yo bro, holding his hand out
Listen up people he shouted
Enjoying the show, he pause
Cool.. Okay come on let's go What ya thought this is free? Nothing is free my man! Three dollars, and while you're at it you can kindly remove all jewelry watches earrings and new sneakers from your person.

The gang ripping off people, roughing them up as they go through the crowd. Four blocks away on the corner Ace has some of his high school girls standing on the corner selling their bodies, while he and Little Rock watch them from across the street inside his 98 oldsmobile Ace rolls down his car window and sticks his head half way out a silk apple red outfit and a Godfather hat to match deck out in Gold. Gold necklace rings and bracelets. Ace raising his voice Come on girls, you don't look sexy to me.
They look alright to me Little Rock said.

Without a doubt, but I want my car customers to be foaming at the mouth Ace reply. Hmmmmmmmmm......

Ace sticks his head back in inside the car, looks at Little Rock and smiles,

have you heard what's been sweeping through town? Rock asked.

Yeah, what I heard sounds pretty good. But its not for me.

Ace takes his hand and straighten out his hat. So when are you going to sign up Ace asked.

Who me?

of course you,

You used to workout Ace reply,

yeah but that was two years ago Rock said.

Look, they say muscles have a memory beside don't you want to make something out of yourself?

so reply Rock.

So sign up for the contest.

But how about you, don't you want something?

said Rock.

Yeah, of course that's why I'm here! Blushing as he fixed his tie.

You know what I mean Rock said as he smile.

Look, Little Rock, this community is for the dogs. You know it, and I know it. As a matter of fact, everybody knows it. So whatever you can do to get out, hey by all means, get out. Remember, it doesn't matter how you get out as long as you get out.

Like high school, it doesn't matter how you get your diploma as long as you get it. Ace stated.

Rock smiling yeah I guess you're right, Reply Rock.

You know, when I think about it I kinda miss high school, I still remember cheating on every test Ace said.

Rock smiling yeah right, we never got caught he reply. We had some strange bugged out people back in those days. Ace said.

I'm telling you,

Remember Wanda? Rock shouted,

Hey, there was nothing strange about Wanda. That was a fine, breathtaking Puerto Rican kid, Ace snapped.

Yeah I must agree, I guess the reason I thought she was strange is because she wouldn't kiss at the prom. Rock reply

How could she? You were too busy dancing with all the other girls like a fly around shit. They laugh hey, remember in high school there was this guy who thought he was a super hero (they both let out a loud laughed) hah! That shit used to crack me up, he used to say I believed in Peace, Justice, and the American way. Remember that shit

Ace shouted. Yeah! He was kind of crazy Rock reply. He used to always try to help people out. No matter who you are if you're in some kinda trouble and he was around he was right there "hey you okay, Is there anything I can do to help? That mother fucker was serious about that shit Ace said.

Yeah, you know its kinda funny alot of people view him as such a nice guy, but he looked more like an angry jeannie.

(Ace and Rock Blushing)

I wonder whatever happened to him, Rock stated.

I wonder if he still lives out here. Ace said.

Nah, I doubt it. Even if he does, he's probably dead and gone because nowadays, the gangs rome the streets and those kats from the projects are crazy. Crime rate is up, that shit, it's higher than inflation,

In a Blushing giggle way they both bust out laughing,

But for real tho knowing him, he probably tried to help prevent somebody from getting mugged, robbed, or something and the wrongdoers probably took him out Rock said.

Yeah right.... What was his name? Grrrrrrrrrrrrrrrrrrr!!! Ace replied.

I don't know, Ace but he was a life saver, Ace reached in the glove compartment and pulls out a 45 Magnum yeah, but I have my own life saver right here and it's on the one. Little Rock was surprise

"oh crib" Rock shouted.

And it will protect me and my girls.

While reaching in his pocket he pulled out a blunt and presses the cigarette lighter button Ace looks at Rock

Oh, it's not program to protect you.

Ace then pulled the chamber back and release it the chamber it Slams back until. It locks.

Now you're. Protected Ace said.

Meanwhile the girls on the corner looking very sexy with blue lipstick on coming up the block are the lord of gangs, The Eliminators. Rock spotted the gang through the side view mirror.

Looks like we have some customers Rock Said.

Ace glance at his rear view mirror and observed several eight members to be exact. Yeah right!

The gang rolled up on the girls,

Hey girls, my boys were telling me that your having a clearance sale said one member.

There was a paused the girls got together,

what's that? One girl reply.

Two for the price of one. He said

He snap his finger and they grab the girls. And takes them into the building. Ace and rock step outside the car, they we're grab by two gang members. Then all the girls came running out of the building screaming. The to members who grab Ace and Rock turned and looked, The members of the Eliminators, whom took the girls into the building, came flying through the front door and the others through the window. While they were watching their fellow members being toss around, Rock and Ace elbow the two members fighting them off. Then Ace pulls out his 45 Magnum and the gang spilts, running down the block. Members yelling as they stumbleing down the block One member yell out

Oh shit, the other

yo come on,

Ace and Rock look at one another

I wonder what happen? said Rock.

Yeah right! Replied Ace.

They race across the street towards the building.

You girls stay right here. Ace said.

As he and Rock running up the stoop, Ace and Rock enter the building cautiously, they proceeded up the inside staircase. Meanwhile the girls are outside frightened and concern for Ace's and Rock's safety. A couple of minutes later, Ace and appears at the third story. Window where some of the gang members were thrown. Looking out of the window

"Whatever it was, we didn't even get a chance to say thanks. Ace stated.

Little Rock started looking around and spots a bucket of water.

Look,

Ace turns around

Maybe the janitor had something to do with this.

The janitor turn his baseball cap backward while mumbling to himself, as he goes down the hall mopping the floor.

Yo what the fuc' is that his back? Rock said softly.

Those damm punks shit, I know the next time I catch somebody on my wet floor.

Rock and Ace look down to their feet. The floor is wet Rock looks at Ace, Ace looks at Rock. Then without any hesitation, they both race down the stairs out of the building.

Hey, this isn't for me. There has got to be a better way. This is not my will to be like this Rock said.

What about that contest? I am sure you can do it, the only thing you will need is for someone to take sometime out to coach you along the way Reply Ace. yeah, maybe your right. Rock sign.

Of course I am right, Mr. Gee was always right. Even though he was a M.F.

(they both laugh)

But seriously Rock, he was always saying to you in gym if you just focus you can be or achieve anything, just like when you're on the throne you can make shit happen.

Yeah but, Rock said, he was always joking around.

Maybe he wasn't stated Ace. (Rock looks at Ace)

He could have been on the up and up.

(Rock still staring at Ace, thinking)

Perhaps you're right. It's worth a shot.

They started down the steps leading to the sidewalk.

Yeah what do I got to lose.

Hey I know the stakes are high, but if you don't make it, you can what huh, always come back here and help me out.

(They stop walking)

It will be like beef steak Charlie. I'll bet they

(pointing at the girls)

can make you say uncle.

(Ace and Rock laugh)

sounds good, listen I have to go turn some burgers,

(They shake hands)

later on bro,

(the girls running towards Ace as Rock leaves. They all grab holding Ace.

Acey baby, I'm scared, one girl said.

Don't be afraid my pets, Acey baby will protect you. Now how's about given Acey baby a kiss. Mmmmm, hun, hmmmm, okay, nice, nice.. Now go on, go go, walk over to the next corner and make Acey baby some money OK, don't look at me like like that in a convening tone move baby! Come on now just a few hundred dollars more my love's Ace shouted.

You're ain't right! One girl quickly shouted, you're not right Ace we're tired we need a break..

I ain't right, what huh, I ain't right! My pockets ain't right.

He pause then he pointed at her

you ain't right, fix your hair woman, I'll Break my foot off

He started to raise his right leg no, no he said to himself not that leg that's the bad foot, that's my bad foot. As the girls walking down the block, Ace gets into his car.

CHAPTER TWO

At McDonald parking lot a vehicle pulls up in front of the restaurant. Big-D gets out of the car and enters the restaurant. It was very crowded but the lines was moving fast before D, knew it he was next on line. The cashier said in a well manner tone,

Next in line. D, step up,

Welcome to McDonald's she said.

And in a firm voice directly to the cashier he said

Hello, ah, I want two mac's and a shake!

The cashier was Blushing,

what flavor?

As her head raised from his nabbed to his face.

In a demanding voice

Strawberry!

Because the tone in Big D voice, the smile quickly left the cashier face. At that particular moment, everyone in the place looks up to see who is the guy that's possess this powerful voice. They stare for a while, and eventually returned to what they were doing. Big D paid the cashier and say

Thanks!

with that powerful voice of his and he exits, A co-worker shouted

damm! Did your saw That tall big mother fucker,

okay, okay it's over people. Back to work..

In the kitchen area of McDonald Rock is looking up at the clock on the wall.

Man, it's a quarter to four, I feel like clocking out now. I'm tired and my feet hurts..

It's only three forty five, you got fifteen more minutes and besides, you can't leave this early anyway.

His co-worker reply

Huh, play on words Rock answered.

As he grabs his bag's punches his time card, his time card, and heads for the door. Just before leaving, he turns and say,

Oh yeah, if the boss asks where am I tell him I'm in the bathroom or something. You know how to hook it up, you lie good anyhow.

They both laugh as Rock exit the restaurant bound for home... As he approached Greenland park, he began to pause, knowing that the park is ran by a gang called the CONDORS, he proceeds with caution. While jogging through the park, he is spotted by one of the gang member's. He shouted out to Rock

Hey you, hey,

Rock then turns to find himself being tailgated by all the gang land members. Focusing on the pipes and baseball bats that they, were carrying, Rock whispers a little prayer, to himself. Then without any hesitation, he takes off in flight and from that point on the big chase began. Two of the gang member's caught up to little rock causing him to stop and do battle. With not a minute to lose, Rock swings his tote bag hitting the nearest gang member to him. Realizing that the other gang members are closing in on him fast, Rock quickly looks around trying to seek his way free. Seeking an opening, he races toward it, but is caught by a fist to the face which stagger rock, sending him to the ground. Many kicks and punches followed. While on the ground Rock manages to avoid being hit by the baseball bats and pipes. Able to get to his feet, he quickly dashed through the brushes leaving the gang a good distance behind as they trailed in hot pursuit. Ski shouted out at his member's catch him and fuck him up.

Rock, almost out of the park, begins to show signs of exhaustion. The same two gang members, who caught up to him before, we're closing in on him once again. Looking nervously, Rock spots a 2x4 wooden block about the length of a baseball bat. He reaches down and grips it with both hands. Just then Rock hears a noise, and with quick reflexes, he swings the 2x4 smashing one member in the face. Sending him to the ground. Still finding himself tailgated by more members of the gang, Rock takes off again.

Then out of nowhere appears this big 6'6 gang member Moose, Moose is holding a street metal pole with a sign attached to it. Rock, stopping a few feet in front of him, is petrified as he watches this big monster grin at him, attempting to swing the stop sign with the green pole attached to it in Rock direction. Moose is caught by a blow that sends him flying to the ground. The blow came from a 6'9" person. Rock doesn't know, as of yet, who this other person is until the person turns around. Focusing on the rest of the gang member's as they began to close in on them. The big guy, grabs Rock and says

Come on man, we got to get you out of here.

They both ran toward a car parked a few yards from them. The big guy and rock both jumped in before the gang could get close enough to do any bodily damage. And with not a moment to spare, they skidded off and faded in the distance. In the car Rock, holding his eye, reaching inside his bag and pulls out a napkin, looking surprised

I know you now, you were the guy in the restaurant, McDonald making all that noise.

Are you always that courteous?

Only when I'm in a good mood. Big-D replied.

You saved my neck back there, I could have handled a couple of the other guys, but that big 7'9' dude, forget it.

Glad to be of some help. I only help those who are in the right and I think he was too much for you to handle by yourself. By the way what's your name?

Daniel better known as Little Rock, but you can call me Rock for short.

Yeah well my name is D,

D for Darryl but they call me Big D

Rock cut him off I understand clearly D made a right turn. So what do you do? I mean, because you look pretty big I can tell you workout, you a boxer?

Nah man, I'm into bodybuilding but I want to become something much more than a person with a body,

D looked kinda puzzel at Rock,

I mean someone different.

Different, like a demi-God? D asked.

They both laugh

I can't really but it into words.

I know what you are trying to say you want to become someone that made a difference not just another person with a body that made the build boards, but someone that the youths can look up to especially the ones who have talent but feel they can't achieve their goals because of where they live or the color texture of their skin. I get it Rock. D said.

Now don't get me wrong I like other sports too. Like football, basketball, and yes boxing and girls, But bodybuilding will always be number one for me. Rock said.

Well 'that's cool. By the way, where do you live?

A few blocks down, on Mott avenue. they turn off on central avenue heading toward Mott avenue. D reaches over and turns the radio on, the volume was low D turn it up a little, the first station is broadcasting the 24 hour news, cops are looking for a group of youths who's been spray painting cars windshields at traffic lights. D change the station, a commercial is on he changes it again and there's another commercial playing. So he turns it off, he then slows down for the light. At the traffic light front of the 101 pct. Rock said

I've been thinking, I am going to need a trainer. Someone to help me correct me if I make any mistakes. Do you know anyone? how about you D, you look pretty strong and knowledgeable about taking care of your body.

Nah, I'm not much of a coach or anything you know, although, I want to see you reach your goal and everything,

pausing for a second, D is thinking hard who he know would help out.

Meanwhile a car pulls alongside of D with dark tinted windows two teenages, both laughing, attempted to spray some paint on D windshield. With both hands grabbing the back of the front passenger chair and pull himself up, yo hurry up before a officer comes out, the back seat passenger yelled out'. The driver placing his finger to his lips I think we got a live one.

The driver press the button lowering the window of the front passenger window,

go ahead man, do it.

The teenager holding the spray can outside of the car, stares up at the light waiting for it to turn green.

I got this man lay low man hey, bust the move just get ready to go in flight.

Just then Big D looks over to his left and sees the teenager. The light turn green, however the expression on D's face quickly discourage the teen. The driver shouted.

What's up man? lights green, come on let's do it, do it man do it.

With a scared look on his face

Oh no, go!!!!! go, come on get outta here!!!! go!!!!

The driver takes off they made a left at the light on cornaga ave and fade into the distance, almost hitting a telephone pole. Big D shaking his head as he kept straight making a right at the second stop sign.

Driving down the block, D said

Listen, I know a guy who's a close friend of mine. He can probably help you out ok, I'll keep in touch.

Yeah' cool, I really appreciate it and especially for what you did back in the park. Rock reply.

Oh, it was nothing. Like I said before, I always look out for people who are in the right you know it's no problem.

D makes a right turn. Rock pointing

I live over there.

D pulls up to the house where Rock live,

Well, looks like this is where I get off.

Rock gets out of the car and stand next to it.

Thanks again for everything and I'll see you around.

Big-D begins to pull off slowly when Rock remembers something and shouts out to him.

Oh yea, what about that guy you were telling me about?

Shouting back while driving off I'll let you know.

Rock takes his keys out and opens the door. He walks inside, takes his jacket off and throws it on the couch. He then turns on the radio, kicks off his shoes and heads for the refrigerator to pour himself a glass of apple juice. He drinks while he's snapping his fingers to the music. After finishing his drink, he goes into the bathroom to brush his teeth. While taking the top off the toothpaste, Rock stares into the mirror at himself.

Mj said it's starts with the man in the mirror, Hmmmmmmmm.

Looking seriously

I'm gonna be the best, I'm gonna. be the best, I'm going to be the best.

As he is saying this he clinches his fist tighter and tighter not realizing, until looking down, that he had squeezed the toothpaste all over the bathroom sink, looking at it, then to himself in the mirror, he smiles and says

Oh!! What the heck.

Leaving the the bathroom, he entered the bedroom. Takes out a pair of pj's from the dresser draw and throws them upon the bed. He takes off his shirt and stands before the mirror in his room pointing to the mirror at himself,

you are the best

he pause for a quick moment then he said...

Word!

And at that instant he drops down and started doing push ups.

CHAPTER THREE

The next day the sun shining through the windows of Rock house the shower water running there is a knock at the door, the knock sounds again, the shower water stops. Rock hears the knock the third time and shouted.

Just a minute.

He comes out putting on his bathrode and shouts who is it? shouting back it's me me Big D, open up.

Rock opens the door while still drying his hair. Big D steps in Good news while walking pass rock who is still holding the door open in suspense. Closing the door, Rock walks into the dining room area finding D staring all around nice place you got, by the way, got anything to eat?

sure, in the frigg, help yourself.

Big D walks over to the refrigerator Rock asks,

what's this you were telling me, when you walked in? Big D heads is way in the ice box oh yeah, I found the guy's number while going through my glove compartment.

Stuffing a few seedles green grapes in his mouth.

By the way, how badly do you want to do this?

what do you mean

Rock said while drying his hair with the towel.

I'm talking you, you making it with your bodybuilding, are you serious man, because it's hard out there and do you know why it's hard out there? I'm tell you why because if it was easy then I'm sure everyone who have a desent shape would be doing it, but it's more than just being in shape every muscle must speak volume... And another thing who's gonna want to give you a chance, listen first of all you're black, second of all this isn't that boxing movie this shit is real. The competition is very heavy and they all have the same dream and the same goal you have. Listen dreaming is one thing, saying it is another, but making it come true is something else. Believe me Little Rock because I've been there, so are you really serious or what? now I'm not talking about killing yourself you can stay where you at if you even thinking about that route, you have guy's who's taking the quick way to stardom. Who don't want to work hard from the core to accomplish this goal. And they will pay for it even if it cost them their lives. They want to see their names in bright lights, have females screaming their name out dying to sleep with them sigining authograpphs, if you're one of these guy's then I'm outta here after I finish eating. I don't mine going to church not funerals. So I ask you again how badly and are you serious? D reply.

I'm serious D, I'm willing to go through whatever I have to and yes from the heart not from the needle or pills.

I like that

D said while he stuff a couple of more grapes in his mouth waving the phone number in his hand he reaches for the phone and starts dailing Q-tee the trainer. with a mouth full of grapes.

Oh yeah you will have to quit your job. And... by the way I'm using your hello Q-tee yeah this is D

I got this kid that wants to make it. In bodybuilding yea he's good and hungry, Q you know you owe me one, yea I know so is he straight or what, yeah okay later....

D hangs up the phone. He turns to Little Rock and says,

Now stop dreaming...... Let's start doing it...

The Next Day a nice sunny warm day expanding on the environment over looking houses and streets of Mott avenue looking down on parks and street corners with the boom box playing loud. A full court game of intense basketball is being played, girls holding conversation and little kids jumping around. Little Rock is doing push ups as D count them. Some guy's came over and disturbing the count by questioning Rock one asked

what the hell are you doing?

others asks whats going on?

another guy ask why are you training,

And with a mad expression, D tells them what they can do and where they can go.

Look guys Rock is training for a contest and he doesn't want to be bothered okay, and right now you all are making my skin crawl so if you disturb him again, I'm going to break your face comprendo?

The brothers chill out they all replied back

okay D take it easy, clam down, as they walk away. Big D got right back on counting 46 47 48 49 50

Rock just finished 50 when D said do 50 more and Rock went back down one two three replied D...

Just then Q-tee walks through the gate look, here comes Q-tee, Rock started to look then D shouted

look with ur mind not your eye's.

Q-tee the coach,walks over to them,shakes D hand and say what's up.

Big-D replied 20, 21 22 23, what's up 26 27 28 Q look down at Little Rock yeah, Q this is Rock we call him little rock because no matter how much he eats 50, D shouted. He just can't gain a pound they both smile.

Rock jump up, Q-tee this is the guy I was talking about over the telephone.

Q shakes Rock hands so you want to become a body builder?

Yes that's what I want to do. That's my goal

Rock picks up his towel and they all begin to walk out the gate.

Q asked

Are you willing to go the distance? I mean, this is no easy road. You have got to sweat it. You're got to to work until every muscle in your body aches and you must learn to over come any and all obstacles that gets in your way. Like sex! He shouted, get some soon so you can remember what it's like, because for the next few weeks, you will have officially retired from that sport. You can't afford to waste or lose any energy. I'm sure you are familiar with the saying winner's never quit and quitters never win.

They stopped next to Big-D car come on, I want to show you something.

They get inside the car and D, droves off.

CHAPTER FOUR

Arriving at the gym

Not knowing where he was going Rock eye's open up real wide when D pulled up at the gym a place he only saw in his dreams and in magazines. They walk inside. Most of the guy's were working out on some of the equipment, mainly the weights and speed bags. Others were jumping rope while dress in karate gees. Big-D taps Rock on the shoulder Rock turns around, D points at the guy's in karate gees.

If you get into a little bit of that those guys from the gang wouldn't be bothering you.

Rock looking puzzled while watching the two guys in karate gees.

Don't worry kid, it just looks difficult D said.

They walked to the back of the gym to an office.

So how do you like the place Q asked

hey looks pretty good Rock reply.

Good! Welcome aboard, sign your name here on the registration form Q hands Rock a piece of paper.

When you finish that, I'll show where your locker is, by the way get some rest and tomorrow be ready for work, Rock signs the form and hands the form paper back to Q-tee and they all walk towards the door

And D, take care of him and make sure he does the right things. Remember, starting now he is in training.

They began to walking out.

Oh and little rock, Rock turns around you better bring that towel.

They exit the gym walking back towards the car Big-D spots a hot dog stand.

I don't know about you, but I'm hungry, I can go for a hot dog, how about you?

Yeah! Why not make mine with everything.

Rock goes and waits in the car while Big-D is ordering. D comes back with the two hot dogs, as he walks over to the driver side of the car, Rock leans over and pushes the door open for him. As the door swings open hard, it almost hits D in the leg this cause him to lose his balance a little and he almost drops the food, he hands Rock his frank and soda. Just then the vehicle door swings on the rebound and hits Big-D on the back of his legs sending his food flying out of his hand on to the street. D looks down at it for a moment, then angrily D sighs as he gets into the car. During this time Rock is trying very hard not to laugh, however a few giggles do manage to slip out. D turns look at Rock and then snatches his frank.

What are you doing?

Rock shouted oh, I'm just looking out for you little bro, just looking out and besides you're in training anyway. They pulled off.

Rock's House

The telephone rings Rock picks it up. It's duke, Rock's friend.

What's happening Rock? I tried to reach you earlier, but you wasn't home.

Oh I was out at the gym getting thing's together, you know for the contest.

Oh, hum...

Rock about the contest, you're be playing by yourself home boy Duke said.

What do you mean?

I mean I won't be able to participate in this contest because, well you see I don't quite have myself together as far as pumping. I've been studying alot for college and I don't have time to work out.

Wow man, and we had it planned to go in this together and now your booking off to college Rock said

Hey man, get yours because I can always get into that a little later, but right now I want to experience this college scene, where the teacher's are mean and the powerful girls run around in blue jeans now, don't get me wrong, I'm still down for body building. As a matter of fact, I'll be there to cheer you on when you win.

Yeah man I know but still

The door bell rings and Rock yell out

Who is it?

It's Marie Rock girlfriend

It's me Marie

Hold on Duke Rock lays the telephone down on the couch and goes to open the door.

Hi Marie said as she walks in and little rock welcomes her with a kiss as he closes the door.

I'm glad you came over. I was going to call you, oh I'm on the phone. Why don't you plant yourself and I'll be with you shortly. Marie walks into the living room taking off her sweater while Rock returned to the telephone. Inside the living room, Marie walks over to the couch and sits down. Suddenly pain flows through her stomach, Marie, holding her stomach, revealed an ugly expression. Showing the suffering that she is going through. Busy on the phone, Little Rock is unaware of what is going on.

Hello Duke, oh I'm sorry Marie was at the door.

Hey Rock, check it out, I've got to split, but remember homeboy it's out there and the only thing you have to got to do is to reach out and get it. Give them a piece of the rock and I don't mean prudential. Duke replied.

Ahh yeah! Shouted Rock.

So you chill out and I'll rap to you later.

Alright partner, later on little rock hangs up the phone. Marie straightens up quickly before little rock walks into the living room. Entering the room, Rock turns toward his girlfriend.

This is it baby, I'm telling you this is it. Rock shouted.

This is what? Marie asked.

Rock walks around the room

Are yeah, finally little by little my dream is beginning to come true Rock said looking up at his picture and shaking his head back and forth.

What are you talking about? Marie said

You wouldn't believe what happen. He shouted. I met this guy name Big-D and I mean he is really big. He helped me find a coach who is really going to help me to reach the top. The coach name is Q-tee, this is it love our street call straight.

He pause

But I ain't counting you know.

you met who?

Big -D and what Q-tee?

who are they drug dealers? Marie asked.

Nah baby Q is my coach and my advisor, D is my Bodyguard babe.

I'm so happy for you Rock I have a real good feeling you're going to make it Marie said with so much confident.

Yeah, that's what everybody else is saying.

Yeah, but I am not everybody else. Marie replied,

Then little rock sister, cookie, comes out of her room buttoning up her coat.

oh hi Marie.

hi Cookie.

Cookie turning toward little rock Little Rock, I'm leaving now, I'll be back tomorrow so take care.

she kisses him, then said and don't forget to water the plants and feed the fish ok. I'll see you on Friday little brother.

Good bye Marie. she walks out the door.

Bye cookie Marie repiled.

She pause for a moment

Little Rock I have faith in you and I know you'll achieve that goal you're striving for.

Marie gets up,walks over to Rock and she puts her arms around his waist

I know because I love you and I believe in you little rock, I really do and I know you can do it.

she pause again then quickly she said with the lord on your side and with my love vibrating in your heart, reminding you and letting you know that, Marie begins to show her feeling toward little rock, I am with you everystep of the way.

I really do love you too Marie,

Little Rock and Marie kiss with alot of feeling behind it nice and slow Kisses, Kiss,

Mmmmmmmm Huh! Marie

Marie reaches her hand out and place her finger on Rock's lips and then she said

Sh, Sh, Sh,

Then they continue on letting their emotions flow. Then Marie realize she is late for work.

Ooh, ooh, oh my goodness, I am so sorry little rock, but I have to go, I'm late for work.

So quickly she kisses little rock twice, pick up her sweater and her pocket book and heads toward the door.

Do you have to go?

he ask as he follow down the hall after her. Rock stops her at the door.

Yeah I have to, I'm sorry.

Well, at least can we have dinner tonight Rock asked

That will be splendid, I get off at 8 o'clock O'k

Great, I love you

Marie reaches over and kiss Rock and quickly says

I love you too. I am running late. I got to go.

She leaves as Rock close the door. He enter the kitchen, and he begins to prepare the food for tonights dinner.

Chapter Five

At rock house the night of the dinner.The door bell rand,little rock answered by saying who is it?

It's marie little rock,

Rock opens the door and feast his eyes on the way marie looks, well can I come in?

Rock still amazed, has a delay reaction. Then finally realizing what was said he quickly answered.

Oh yeah I'm sorry it's just that you look so beautiful and so extremely lavishing tonight

As he welcomes her in.

Well you look very neat yourself marie said.

Rock tells Marie to close her eyes so he can surprise her about the dinner table. Marie eyes are close, well it's just a little something I put together. Now close your eyes oh okay your eyes are already close cool he smile, Rock takes her hand and leads her to the dinning room area, and behold he shouted okay open your eyes now.

Marie opens her eyes and was very surprised at the way little rock had arranged the dinning room area. A candle light dinner, champagne, a bottle of Ruinte peach table wine, and soft music, Marie is so amazed that she doesn't know what to do.

Oh, Little Rock

Marie can't believe her eyes, she turns to little rock and throws her arms around him and kiss him.

Everything is so romantic and lovely

she said softly as she looks around with sparkling watery eyes in fascination.

Wait until you taste it

Rock said he pulls up a chair for her to sit down. Then turns on some soft music by Kenny G.

Aww yeah! he said

as he comes back to the table he reaches in his pocket and pulls out a match and lights the candles. Then he turns the lights off and return to the table. Once he is seated, he looks at Marie and says,

You look so pretty.

Just for you, always and forever until death do we apart.

Reply Marie. Then the song always and forever comes on. Marie eyes filled with love and tears.

I love you so much,.... So much that someday, hey I ain't counting, but I would like you to someday be my wife.

Marie expression on her face was priceless she were very surprised her feelings for Little Rock has scale from a 5 to a 10 just that quick, it couldn't go no higher because the scale only went up to 10.

In a sweet lovely way she said

I would love to Little Rock and I promise I'll be a good wife and I know you'll make a wonderful husband.

Rock smile

I'll try my best too, to please you, for you will be my heart and I'll be your Inspiration and part of your strength. The out come of this will bring about love, Honesty, Peace, Happiness and Joy. we'll live each and every day to it's fullest extent with the Lord Jesus Christ at the beginning of each day. We will not become just a plant, but the supreme creature that God intended us to be.

Rock reaches out and grabs Marie's hand then he kissed her. Afterward they stared at each other with a strong feeling that Samson can't break.

Well let's have a toast.

They lift up their glasses and placed them close to each other without touching

May our dreams come true, although, it may rain sometimes never fret for on the other side of the rainbow lies the key, and baby we're going to make it.

The glasses touch. They began to have dinner.

Now in the middle of their dinner, Marie requests to dance.

OOH,... That's my favorite song.

yeah, it is Rock replied.

yeah, come on let's dance.

Dance! Rock said

Marie reaches her arm out and grabs his hand.

Yeah, come on

He get's up and they walk into the living room and began to dance. while dancing Marie says

you know I love you

looking up at Rock.

Rock Looking down at her

I love you too.

Then the two love birds kiss and continue to dance.

You know we have the house all to ourselves. Just you and I Rock said.

Yea, that's the way I like it just you and I crowds don't interest me at all.

Rock Blushes as they dance on. Then all of a sudden Marie begins to get weak and starts to stagger around.

Little Rock, I feel funny, sort of nauseous.

she stop dancing. Rock is very concern

what's wrong baby?

I don't know, I just want to lie down suddenly she faints. Rock catches her, picks her up in his arms and takes her to the bedroom.

I got you baby don't worry everything will be alright.

He get's to the bedroom and yells at peables, his dog to move off the bed. Rock then lays Marie down on the bed.

I got to called the emergency room.

Rock opens up Maries blouse, so she can get some air.

Just hang in there baby you'll be alright.

He turns to the phone to call the emergency room. As he begins to dial the number, he hear a voice, Little Rock,.... Little Rock,

Rock turns to the bed where Marie laid, but she was gone. Then he heard the voice again. Rock then turns around to find out where the voice is coming from and there in front of him, to his surprise, stands Marie looking more beautiful than ever dressed in cookies night gown.

Well, how do I look? Rock caught by the elements of surprise, drops the receiver on the floor.

You look lovely, but I thought you were sick replied Rock.

Oh, I am sorry little rock.

As she tried to explain she walks slowly towards Rock. Then stands in front of him,

You really do love me. You really do care for me alot and I am very great full.

Marie place her arm's around Rock neck and Rock place's his arm's around Marie's waist.

Little Rock, I want to be very honest with you. I've never experienced, you know love before. I've always kept it to myself, but now I want to share it with you. Marie kisses Rock as they lean back onto the bed.

CHAPTER SIX

It's the next day, the scene fades to the window at the ray's of the sun. Then back to the bed where Marie lays asleep. Rock enters the room with his sweat suit on, sits on the bed and begins to put on his sneakers. Waiting outside is Big-D. Yo Rock he yell, then he whistles, yo Rock.

Rock reaches over and kisses Marie.

I'll see you when I get back.

Sleepy as Marie was she barely woke up. Just as Rock is about to leave Marie calls him back.

Little Rock,

Rock turns around and crawls on the bed into Marie's arm's.

Yeah baby. I love you she said

Marie begins to tear,

I love you too Marie oh no, no no, why are you crying? Was I too rough or too hard I mean too aggressive last night?

Marie smile

No just hold me, please hold me.

Rock holds Marie in his arms.

Little Rock I'm scared, but I love you. What's happening little rock what's happening?

Marie breaks down in tears Rock holds her a little tighter.

It's okay Marie I am not going to let anyone or anything hurt you okay? Rock said. Marie shakes her head alright. Big-D getting impatience

Yo Rock, what's up? Let's go.

I have to go,

Rock kisses Marie, Peables jumps onto the bed.

Later peables, good bye baby.

Rock dashes out quickly he gets downstairs to Big-D.

What's up man? You know we have to be at the gym at seven o'clock. This kat Q- is one of those on time coaches.

They walk to the car and take off for the gym.

At The Gym

Knowing that they are late, Rock and Big-D walk inside.. Q was mad where in the hell,have you been? No matter if D was running late or caught in traffic, you hit the pavement. You know this is important. I said seven o'clock and you come walking in here at seven thirty five.

Q points at Rock,

Look, if you keep this up don't bother coming. Now, over there is the lockers

Q points at the far corner

Your number is twenty six.. Let's do it.

Rock headed towards the lockers... In the middle of the work out. Rock working on bench press with his Manger coaching him as Big-D looking on. Q yelling come on push it, feel the pain, come on three more. Let it out Rock finishes the set. How do you feel?

Rock looks up at Q as the pain vibrate through his chest his expression tells it all,

Good! We've just begun Q turns away come on Rock turns around on the bench and then lay down facing the opposite position. Rock is doing flyers with 35lbs dumbells six, seven, eight, nine, ten, ten more, push! I don't deal with needles pills or that other shit. That's all temporary, hard work dedication sweat blood and tears that's what true champions are all made of and you are going to be one of them.

Rock pulling up his last rep push!!! Q shouted......

Meanwhile at Maries house two months later. Marie comes home, but home was unlike she has ever seen it before. As she opens the door she saw the reason why, boxes everywhere. Marie momentarily looks around, puzzle, then she let's her mother know that she is home.

Mom I'm home.

She heard noise in the kitchen area. Marie walks into the kitchen

Hi Mom.

Marie's mother turns her head as she rinses off the cabbage.

Don't hi mom me

Marie's mother drops everything as she places her hand on her hips.

Where in the hell have you been? Don't you know I've been worried about you?

Yes mother

Marie puts her head down. Here I am worried sick, thinking that someone has kidnapped you or that your lying out there dead somewhere. Where have you been?

Marie raises her head up slowly.

I was with little rock.

The expression or Marie mother's face was priceless.

Who?

little who?

Little Rock.

Who in the hell is little rock?

He's my boyfriend momma.

Your boyfriend, you mean to tell me you're been with that punk all night and he didn't have the decency to bring you home. Girl, when are you going to learn, they meaning boy's including Mr. Little Rock they all the same.

Marie mother continues on while washing the cabbage.

They only want you to help them support their habits.

Oh no momma, little rock is different. He's an original. He told me That he loves me.

Marie's mother smiles as she puts the pot on the stove.

With the name little rock, sure he does. What mother would name their child little rock. Listen honey, they will tell you anything in order to find out the name of the company that makes your panties.

Marie walks around in the kitchen.

Mother his name is Daniel his friends called him little rock. And well, I believe him and besides I think I'm in love with him.

Marie's mother begins to fix the rice when she smiles.

Love, sugar listen to me,

Marie's mother walks over to the table and sat down.

Your father once told me the same thing. He said, baby I love you.

She went on telling Marie about the experience she had, but marie is so deeply in love that nothing can hindered her love for Rock.

Marie, I don't want the same thing that happened between your father and I to happen to you baby. Don't you understand?

Yes I understand mom, but mom, you don't understand I'm in love with him. We're lovers and there's nothing that can change that.

Marie's mother began to get very angry

look girl, the only thing that you are going to fall in love with is this broom stick up side your head. You're in love, huh girl don't make me curse. This so call little rock, Daniel has got your mind all screwed up.

Marie mother gets up, picks up the garbage and hands it to marie.

Here, fall in love with this garbage. Now do your lover a favor and take him out.

Marie, looking sad, worried, and discouraged. She takes the garbage from her mother and walks out of the kitchen as her mother carries on with her cooking. While outside, Marie begins to have stomach pains again. The pain hurts so badly that she lost her balance and has to lean up against the house. Then she slides down to the ground.

CHAPTER SEVEN

Meanwhile back at the gym..... Q-tee shouting Push,...... Push...... Come on more, get into. You're not getting into it, come on.

Rock straining on the sets of front flyers, he just couldn't take anymore and drops the dumbells on the floor.

What in the hell do you think I am?

A winner!!!

Q quickly replied.

Rock realizes what his manager Q is trying to say.

Now come on, last set and I want ten. D get the forty five.

Big-D picks up, the forty five and hands it to Rock.

Come on!

Rock grabs the dumbells and begins again. This time Rock puts determination into his reps.

Yeah, that's it, feel the pain they're your friends, they know the way to big shoulders, remember it's not how many you do as long as you're doing it correctly and the muscles will respond. Three more, one.. Two.. three, okay here

Q throws rock a towel.

Shower up.

After a good workout, Rock went home. Arriving at his house, Rock opens the door and turns on the lights. Feeling very exhausted, he throws his bag down on the sofa arm and goes into the kitchen to get a glass of orange juice from the refrigerator. Peables walks in with a letter in her mouth.

Peables! Home digger dee, come here girl.

Peables walks to rock. Rock sees the note.

What's this girl?

As he takes the note from peables mouth, he looks at her, Marie left huh.

Rock reads the letter then he understands oh well, hey peables, where's cookie? Go get cookie and bring her here.

Peables runs into the bedroom to get cookie. Cookie is asleep on the bed. Peables then jumps onto the bed and pulls the covers off cookie licking her on the face.

What the, get off the bed.

Peables lick her in the face again

Stop, cut it out.

Peables runs to the edge of the bed barking, she then runs back trying to tell cookie what rock said.

What's wrong dog?

Peables runs off the bed and heads for the door. There she stops and turns around.

Oh, you want me to follow you. Look dog this better be important.

Cookie gets out of the bed, puts on her rode and follows peables. As they approached rock's bedroom, cookie understands

oh, Little Rock wanted me.

But when they came inside, Rock was fast asleep.

Great! Come on you mutt.

Cookie and peables walk out of the room quietly.

Next morning rock wakes up and reaches for the clock on the desk. Realizing the time he yells out

"Oh no!!

Quickly rock gets up out of the bed, sh I were and gets dress. Cookie is down stairs fixing breakfast. The a rumor woke up everybody the birds the squirrels even the the sun shining through the windows wanting to see what's for breakfast. Rock enters the kitchen. Mmmmmmmmmmmmm what's for breakfast sis? Beacons and eggs, light toasts with grape jelly. Then the car horn beeped twice. Sounds good, but I have to go. I'll see you later. He kissed cookie as he walks toward the door he sees peables, later on peables. Peables barks twice as Rock walks out the door.

At the gym rock is on his back routine, Q is pacing back and forth.

Look rock you're not lifting the weights correctly. Let's see, hmmmmmmmmmmm

Q points at the weights

just imagine this is 80 pounds of shit and every time you buckle your elbows it's coming down on you. So to avoid being covered with shit you have to push the shit up ok. Now let's try it again, come on.

Big-D lifts the weight up and hands it to Rock. This time with determination. Rock try it again.

Yeah, that's it, push it up, push, come on.

Rock screams for desire

come on push, push. Ok, put it down.

Rock puts the weight down.

Now, do ten flys.

Q hands Rock two dumbells.

Come on, one, two, three, four, push, five, six, seven, one, come on, two, three, come on, four, five, six, seven, eight, eight, eight...

Hours later after the workout. Q and Big-D waiting for rock to get dress.

Hey Rock, lets go.

Rock rushes to the front door.

I'm coming.

As Rock approach them, big D pulls his jacket over his shoulder and said

come on man. What we're you doing back there?

I was pitting my hair,

Rock fixes his clothes.

What!!!

Big-D pushes rock head. They laugh as they walk out the door. Q joking around with rock as they walk down the block toward the car.

Rock, have you ever realize that it takes years and years to become a professional?

Big-D said.

Yeah, I

Rock get cut off by Q,

yeah I what, you know? You're barely achieve how to pee in a toilet and you know that was hard. judging from your track record, you were the coolest, most accurate, professional bed sheet pisser around. One can just imagine what your bed sheets use to look like.

They laughed

Oh wow, that's really cold blooded. Rock replied.

Q still laughing hold it, seriously, all jokes aside. Little Rock, I don't believe in all those years. And I damm don't believe in Steroids. Not saying it won't work. But why place your life on the line for a career that you might not be around to enjoy. Beside that's temporary. What I am offering is something that's gonna stay what it you like your birthmark. I believed in time... Time is important. The contest is next month, just over 4 weeks from now, and you ain't even ready for some puss let alone the contest. They approached the car. Big-D walks around to the driver side, opens the door gets in and unlock the passenger door. However, if you trust me and let me have the chance to mold your dream, strengthen it, nurse it and change it into reality, we can have you ready within a time frame of just three weeks. But it's all up to you rock. Rock feeling somewhat down, he pauses for a second to dwell on everything Q had just said to him. The pep talk given by Q has restored rock's self confidence and has made him more determine than ever. With a made up mind, starting tomorrow. Q opens the car door, and Big-D folds the seat forward for rock. Better yet, starting now. Rock begins to leave, come on get in said Q.

That's alright, I am starting now.

I'm running home. Rock took off.

Are you crazy?

Do you know how far your house is from here?

But there was no use, Rock was already gone. Q gets inside the car and Big-D pulls off.

While jogging home rock runs into a couple of his so call associates. He didn't stop to chat, but pressed onwards. Still thinking about the pep talk Q-tee just gave him, Rock almost ran pass his best friend Ace. Ace stops him. Ace was making out kissing a girl in his car when he spots rock and he hit the horn and yells hold up man, yo Rock Little Rock.

Rock turns around.

Oh cribs, what's up man?

You... what's going on? Ace asked.

Rock glance at his clothes,

oh, well I got back into lifting.

No way! That's good man.

Yeah, I have a manager now he goes by the name of Q-tee and check this out, I even have a Bodyguard.

Get outta of town! Ace replied.

Man I am more serious than herpes and you know the deal with that.

They laugh as Rock gives Ace some dap.

But word up this brother has hands the size of a baseball mitts and he's about 6'9" tall.

Ace laugh what!

Nah man you're over exaggerated.

Yeah man I'm not lying he's okay if it's not 6'9 it's up there. But hey this feels like this is it Ace. This is my ticket out of this dump. So what you been up to rock asked.

Nothing man,

as he turns around and walks away.

Same old shit, day after day.

Ace walks over to the car.

Rock follow him. Ace beginning to feel depressed and starts breaking. He takes off his hat and throws it down on the street.

I can't take it.

Rock tries to cheer him up.

Hey come on,

Rock grabs Ace by the arm, but Ace is too upset to stand around and reason so he rips his arm away from rock.

Nah rock, I'm tired of the same bull shit over and over, Look

Ace points at the females in his car,

see this shit?

Look real deep what do you see?

I'll answer that nothing but shit!!!

Not the girls. I'm tired of this Rock, I'm no pimp.

Ace opens his car door and tells the girls to leave.

Get out!!! Get the fuc out of my car.

As the girls are getting out of the vehicle, they rebel

Well I never!! Said one girl

You couldn't Ace replied

Two other girls at the same time. Well fuc you!!

Hey look, you're can't talk, you didn't know how until I showed you so shut the fuc up and get the hell away from my car. The girls walk away. go on get away he yell. Hey Ace, relax buddy ok, take it easy man. Are you okay? Rock wipe his hand across his face in a sign of relief.

Yeah.... Ace replied

Okay gotta say tho took alot of guts to do what you just did, I know it must feel good to get it all out off your chest huh,

Yea. Ace replied.

You gonna be okay?

Ace shook his head up and down.

Are you sure?

Hey you know me, fuc that shit man. There has to be a better way Ace opens the car door, gets in and slams the door.

But hey rock go for that man, get yours dude and if you need anything let me know okay. Oh and rock, my father always told me that happiness comes through the achievement of goals so don't make excuses. Don't make the same mistakes I did. Do it, go for it bro and accomplished it.

Rock turns around to leave later man, yeah cool out Ace replied.

As Rock walks away a little boy runs to the car with Ace's hat.

Sir, is this yours?

Yeah, thanks.

Ace goes inside his pocket and pulls out a five dollar bill.

Here go buy yourself something.

Ace, thinking....

CHAPTER EIGHT

At Maries house Mrs Johnson, Marie's mother, is in the dinning room wrapping up her dishes. The house is half empty and Marie is in her bedroom. In a soft but authority tone.

Marie!!..... Marie!! Mrs Johnson called Marie...

Marie comes out of her room to answer her mother Mrs Johnson walks into the living room.

Yes mom. Come on down here and help me with these boxes.

Marie scratches her head as she comes downstairs. Upon arriving downstairs she walks into the living room.

Come on honey, I want to at least pack most of the important things now, so we don't have to worry about them later. I want to get as much as possible out of the way today. In a not willing voice yeah, okay.

Marie begins to help her mother pack the dishes.

I still don't understand why we have to move.

The telephone rings. Marie goes to answer the phone. It's vanessa.

Hello, oh hi vanessa.

Hi Marie, are you all finished packing?

Marie turns and looks around the room well, not really. We still, oh... I might as well say it, I still have to pack the household linens and I haven't even started on my clothes. Sounds like you have alot to do. So how are you and little rock coming along?

Marie placing the wrapped dishes in the box.

Well, so far everything is just great. I know this might sounds like a stupid question, but did you tell little rock that you're moving?

Marie walks over to the table, pulls up a chair and sat down. Before answering vanessa, she takes a deep breath inhaling slowly and exhaling slowly.

No I didn't.

Vanessa in shocked,

you didn't, you didn't tell him.

I'm going to tell him.

When? Vanessa asked.

Whenever I see him. I haven't seen him yet, but when I do I'll tell him.

Marie listen, if I were you, I'll go out and look for him and explain it to him that you will be moving and that you all can't be together anymore.

I can't. I can't just let him go just like that. We've been through alot together and besides.....

Besides what? said vanessa.

I'm pregnant.

She pause, I think I'm pregnant. Vanessa in shock,

you what? Does little rock know? Don't tell me Little Rock doesn't know.

Marie takes another deep breath

no, nobody knows except you.

Marie gets up and walks over to the wall and leans against it.

Vanessa! I am showing. I am

she pause again,

I've been feeling very dizzy at times.

In a very confused and frightened tone of voice,

vanessa, what am I going to do?

Marie there is only one thing you can do and that is to find rock and tell him the truth and I think it is about time that you told your mother also, before she finds out. How many months are you?

Wiping her face I... I don't know.

Didn't you go to the doctor?

No Marie replied.

No!! Well girl you better get motivated.

Yeah, I guess you're right.

Marie, Marie!!

Marie mother yelling out for Marie.

Listen vanessa, I have to go. I'll talk to you later okay.

Okay, do it Marie. And if you need anything, please call me okay.

Okay, thanks vanessa, bye.

Marie waits for awhile and then she hangs up the phone. Still thinking about what vanessa said, Marie leans her back against the wall. All a sudden she is startle by a voice calling her name. Marie's mother calls out Marie's name once again. Roughly this time

Marie!!!

She's getting impatient.

Coming mom,

Marie walks into the kitchen.

Mom I have to tell you something.

Not now Marie, I want to get all these things pack.

Marie holds her head down in sorrow as the tears run down her face. Crying as she tries to wipe her eyes mother, please!!!

Her mother stops what she was doing and looks at Marie.

I am pregnant.

Her mother, without saying a word, stood for a moment in shock. She looked at Marie's face with her mouth open, then she looked at Maries stomach.

The Gym

Big-D and Rock are in the center of the room. Dee is teaching rock about karate.

Now just relax and keep your eyes on your opponent. Let your body move, it knows what to do. Remember it has a brain.

Just then Big D fakes a jab at rock face and kicks him in the mid-section. Follow by a round house kick to the face sending rock to the ground.

See?

Little Rock staggering

yeah, I got the point. Replied Rock.

Speed, timing, and know how. These are the most important substances you must learn.

Rock standing to his feet.

Now remember, think before you do anything. For the life you save may just be your own. Understand?

Yeah rock reply.

Now meditation is also another important ingredient. Concentrate on your opponent. Remember, attack all weak points of the body like so Big-D demonstrates on Rock's body rock couldn't move.

Now if you wanted to, you could make the strong points weak points on your opponents body, like so Big-D, still in motion, smash a thrust b low to rock's chest, sending him to the ground.

Understand?

Little Rock holding his chest.

Yeah...

Okay

Big-D turns around to see what else he can teach rock.

Now We are going to get down.

Big-D turns back around towards Rock,

Rock is still on the ground, he started to get up.

When I get finished with you, those guys will address you as Mr. Little Rock. Rock falls back down.

Now hours has passed and it's night time now Q-tee is spending overtime training rock. Rock is doing squats with sweat pouring down from his body as he does quarter inch squats

Huh,... huh...

Come on, push, down, down, three more. Okay, hold it Rock. How do you feel? Tired? Hungry? Ready to hit the shower? Rock replied.

Tired, yeah word up. Hungry, man I am more hungrier than four brother's and a nice hot shower would feel mighty righteous.

I thought so, we'll I am sorry to disappoint you because we still have work to do. We are now going to enter the pain zone. The goal is ten, come on, one, one, one, two, two, two, three, three, four, four, four, five, five, six, six, seven, seven, eight, nine, nine, nine, come on Rock, nine, six, seven, eight, eight, nine, nine, as Q the manager, calls out the numbers, Rock begins to dig deep down inside himself to find that extra burst of energy.

Ten.

Rock place's the bar back on the rack. Q-tee throws a towel in little Rock's face.

Now that's what I call good squats.

Big-D comes in here I come to save the day, Big-D approaches them with some snacks.

Here handing Q a can of soda and Rock a bottle of apple juice.

See the label 100% juice not 100% vitamin c if you have 100% juice you have 100% vitamin c

Q-tee stated. Afterward, Big-D walks over to one of the benches, sits down and pulls out a big hero sandwich. Realizing that he is being stared at he thinks, then just before taking a bite out of the sandwich, he glances up and says want a piece?

as Rock and Q standing over him with weight lifting bars in their hands.

CHAPTER NINE

At Rock's House the telephone rings. Ring,...... ring,...... ring,.... cookie answers the phone. It's marie. Hello, cookie? Yes cookie answered. This is Marie, how are you doing.

Oh hi Marie, I am a little tired, but other than that I am alright.

That's good, cookie is little rock home?

No

He hasn't come in yet. When he does, I'll tell him you called.

Meanwhile time is winding down. Mrs Johnson already ordered the moving truck and half of her things are already on the truck. Pretty soon they will be ready to pull off. Marie has been looking for Little Rock. She is worried and puzzled.

Marie dash to the streets looking everywhere and asking people have they seen little rock. First place she went after thinking it through was his job at McDonald. They haven't seen him. As Marie was walking down the street, she runs into little rock's best friend Ace.

Hey Ace. She walks up to him, have you seen little rock? I've been looking for him and haven't found him yet. I don't know where he is and I'm worried. Marie begins to break down in tears. Ace embrace her as he tries to cheer her up. Wait a minute, hold up. What's wrong, is he in any trouble or something?

Ace asked. Marie wipes her face. No she pause, but then she starts up again. You see, my mother and I are moving and he doesn't know.

Hey, well that's still ain't no reason for you to be crying. Well hey, I understand that you and rock are real close and that you don't want to leave him. Marie starts crying again.

You don't understand. In a very touching voice. I am pregnant.

Oh shit! Ace shouted.

And I can't find him.

Ace started thinking, well have you checked at the gym. Ace rolls his left sleeve up and looked at his watch. Nah it should be closed. Wow, I wish I can help as Marie wipes her face. But the only place I know of, that rock hangs out is either at the gym or his house. Sorry Marie. Ace stated.

It's okay, thanks. She turns around and started walking home. Then Ace said to her. Hey Marie, wanna lift?

Marie turns around slowly, looks and says

No thank you. And walks away.

Meanwhile little rock return home. He opens the door and peables, his dog, jumps in his arms. Peables! How are you doing girl? Peables barks twice, thanks good. I am tired. Rock walks into his bedroom takes off his coat and places it on the bed. Then cookie walks into his room. Marie called. Cookie said.

Yeah what she say?

Nothing, she just wanted to talk to you. Where have you been?

Training he (paused), I have two weeks you know. Rock replied.

Well, I'm going to bed. Cookie said.

Gino's a neighborhood pizza joint. A group of girls are walking towards gino's. Some members of the Redfern crew are driving around in a car. The car flys by the girl's, then a few feet up the street, the car stops.

Hold it stick, the front passenger said.

Stick is the one that's driving the car.

Hey guys did you all see that Dude said.

The members turn their heads around to take a second look.

Did I see it man I can taste it. Those bitches make my dick foam at the mouth. Bear replied.

One guy in the back seat shouted.

Fuc that! Back this shit up.

Hang on stick reply.

Stick puts the car in reverse and backs up next to the girls.

Yo baby, what's your name? asked Dude.

One of the girls looked at the car and winked her eye while the others just smiled as they chewed their gum. As the girls approached the front of the pizza place, they stopped, looked back at the car, wiggled their fancy and walked on inside. That really encouraged the crew members as they took off, speeding up the block in search of a parking space. They found one and parked the car. All six of them got out and began walking towards the pizza place. As they got closer and closer to gino's, they began saying nasty things like titty, titty, legs, titty, legs, titty, titty.

They opened the front door, walked in and stopped. They look around. They spotted the girls seated in the back, but there weren't any more empty seats. However, bin the sight of the members there were six. They walked towards the girls. Just a table away, the crew members stop in front of three couples sitting down. Dude walks over to one couple.

Get up. He stated. He reaches down, yanks the guy right out of his seat and throws him into the rest of the crew. One member said yo, man what's your problem? They grab him Get the fuck off my sneakers. And punch him in the face, sending him to the floor. Dude looked at the guy's girls you too, come on, get out of there. You're finished right? He grabs the girl, she started to say something, but dude cuts her off. Just shut the fuck up and move it. Dude kicks her. The other couples began to get up, but two of the crew members thought they were moving too slow. So the members decided to lend them a helping hand. Finally the couples leave and the crew sit down. Dude tries to impress the girls by ordering a pie at the snap of a finger. Watch this ladies. Can fonzie do this? Finger snaps. Hey pizza boy, one pie. There was a paused.... nothing happened. Johnny! Dude reply. Johnny gets up and walks over to the counter. The man asked for a pie.

The pizza b oy reply, sorry sir, it's not ready yet. Johnny grabs the boy, snatches him from over the counter and throws him against the wall. Is it ready yet. Huh, huh. Johnny picks him up and throws b him back over the counter. The impact causes the oven door to open and the pie to slide-out. Quickly, the boy grabs a box and catches the pie before it hits the floor. He then turns around and hands it to Johnny saying yes, it's ready, oh and don't worry about the bill, it's on me. Johnny grabs the pie and returned to the table. When he arrives there, he said to dude. Hey dude, it works. He puts the pie on the table. Dude take a slice. Of course. You all eat up, while I go over here and make arrangements for our beds to get warm. Dude gets up and walks over to the girls.

At the gym

In the center of the gym. You said you improved. Well I really don't want to show you this but it's for your own good. In a demanding voice Sit down, D said. Rock sat down. The lights went off, a projector screen came down and then the projector came on. The slides show different days of rock's lessons. Rock watches with great concern. Then embarrassed by his performance, Rock slides down in his seat. Soon the projector stops and on came the lights. I must admit that you have improved.

Improved! I was getting beat down on there. Rock said.

Yeah, but you kept on coming and giving it your all to learn. Learning how to ignore pain is important. You have to practice and rock cut him off. Yeah, yeah, I know. Practice, concentration, focus, power, and all that other jazz.

Remember! You're supposed to be the pain giver, not the pain receiver. Now, what we're going to do is combined the martial arts with the street fighting okay.

Rock stand up.

Okay rock said. suddenly Big-D delivers an unexpected stunning punch to the face of little rock.

CHAPTER TEN

Two weeks later Marie is in her new house in her bedroom lying on the bed. And looking through her photo album at some of the pictures she and little rock took. As she looks at each picture, many wonderful memories of them pass through her mind. All of a sudden, Marie begins to weep as her heart remembers the good times. Trying to get a hold of herself, she wipes her eye's but the tears began once more. She gets up off the bed. Walks over to the window, and looks out hoping that somehow, someway rock would come walking down the block. Thinking about the possibility of losing little rock, Marie turns around and focus on the telephone.

Meanwhile at Little Rock's House, the telephone rings and cookie answers it. Hello, oh hi Marie. Yes, just a minute. Cookie calls out little rock's name. Little Rock..... little Rock. Little Rock comes out of his room and enters the living room to see what cookie wanted. Coming, I'm coming. Rock walks toward cookie.

What?

Telephone. She hands little rock the receiver

Hello

Hello, Marie repiled. Rock looks puzzled.

Who is this?

With a soft sweet voice. It's marie little rock. How are doing?

I'm okay, and you?

Fine she replied. Then there was a paused.

Look Marie

Marie cuts him off. With a caring voice. Please little rock. Please let me say something first. I'm sorry. I know I should have told you sooner,

44

but I don't know why I didn't. Marie begins to cry. I am sorry what else can I say.

Little Rock, feeling the anger beginning to build up inside again, he hangs up the phone on her.

I know good bye! As he slams the phone down. Marie quickly calls back and tries to explain. Ring....... ring........ring....... Little Rock, staring at the telephone. Wonders should he answered it or not. Finally, he picks it up on t he third ring. Hello.

Marie tries to pulled herself together as the tears flow down her cheeks and her heart pounds in pain. Hello she pause, she sniffles, little rock please, just listen to me. I love you little rock (sniffing), I've always did. I would never do anything to hurt you. I tried to tell you. I went looking for you and I couldn't find you. (She's still sniffing) really I tried. You have got to believe me. Marie begins to cry. I wanted to tell you that,.... that I,.... I,... I'm preg..... pregn..... pregnant. She really pours out her heart to him and in the process grabs a hold of his. Because of the crying rock couldn't understand what Marie was trying to say.

What?

Rock paused, what did you say?

I am pregnant. I wanted to tell you.

Why didn't you you tell me? He snapped, I'm sorry did I yelled at you? Tell me why didn't you?

I couldn't find you. I wanted to tell you. I am sorry, I was just too scared to tell you at the time. She started sniffing, then she begins to cry heavily once more.

I love you little rock.

I love you too Marie. I am a father, I mean, I am going to be a father. Marie cuts him off by crying more

Hey, stop crying, it's okay.

It's not okay she yelled. I can't see you anymore. Marie hangs up the phone as she cries on.

Next morning at Rock's House

Rock is in bed, fast asleep, dreaming about today's workout schedule. It begins at 6am with 8 miles of jogging. The birds are outside singing as the ray's from the sun fills the room with sunshine. Rock wakes up, stretching out his arms and yawned. Still not fully awake, he rolls over and focus his eyes on the alarm clock, he realizing that he is late, jumps outta bed, walks into the living room and turns on the stereo. While snapping his fingers to the rhythm of the beat, Rock walks into the bathroom and turns on the shower. Noticing himself in the mirror, he stops, points at himself and say You're a winner. Then smiles. Next he opens the cabinet door, takes out the toothpaste, and toothbrush and begins to brush his teeth. Meanwhile Big-D and Q are outside waiting for rock to come out.

Yo Rock, Hoo, Hoo,. Rock. Coming out of the bathroom with a towel wrapped around his waist, walks into his room. He then hears the call and opens the window.

I'll be right down. Five minutes later, rock, comes rushing out of his house running in place.

Let's do it. Q said

They both take off jogging down the block as the morning escorts their run to there's destination.

Jogging through town

While jogging through town unaware of where they're heading, they end up running through Greenland park which is the turf of the Lynbrook Boy's. As they approached the tree's six members of the gang jumps out at them. Three leaped from a tree and the rest came out from behinded the trees. Rock, his manger, and his and his Bodyguard found themselves half surrounded by the land members. They focus on the pipes and baseball bats that the gang member's were holding in their hands. Ski, the leader, began to laugh then Big-D replied

Don't worry, we can handle them. Rock began to think about how hard he trained and that he can't let nothing stand in his way. He started catching flashback on the times he trained, the straining, the aches and pains that he had gone through. Especially the first time he met up with Lynbrook and Redfern crew. Anger begins to build up inside of Rock.

Ski still laughing with his arms around his girl. Then he stops laughing Hey fellas look, three bitches.

In a very mean voice I got your bitch right here. D points down towards his private part. You want it D said. Ski gets mad as his girl laughs at him.

Rock glances at D and whispers Yo, D Man, Kool out. The gang began to get restless and started twirling their weapons. One crew member shouted.

Come on boss, let's fuck them up.

Then the rest join in. "Yeah come on, worded," ski still pissed off at what Big-D said to him, replied.

You mother fucker!! He pushes his girl away and began walking towards Big-D. He glances at Rock and starts to laugh.

Oh shit. He walks up to rock.

Just look at this sweet bitch. As he rubs his hand down on the braids on Rock's head. Then Rock punch him right in the face which ski went straight down to the ground. Big-D look at Rock and smile, gang went crazy and the fight was on.

During the fight, Q-tee gets stabbed. But nothing serious. Light's flashing on the scene. Police cars rushes through the park and the gang flees.

Meanwhile, after the fight. At the gym rock, knowing that his girl is gone and that she is carrying his child, tried to workout. Rock manager is getting very angry about the way little rock is feeling. As Rock does sit ups, Q-tee coaches.

Come on, more, come on Big-D looking on. Yeah that's it, push it, four more, come on... two more, Okay three minutes. Q-tee shouted.

While Rock is resting, he begins to think about Marie. Daydreaming about her as the three minutes come to an end.

Okay rock, last set, come on. Rock stayed still as if he were sleeping. Yo Rock. Q-tee reached to awake him, but Big-D grabs Q Let him sleep. D said.

CHAPTER ELEVEN

On the street

On the way walking home, Rock runs into some of his friends. As Rock crosses the street. A van pulls up What's up little rock? Ace asked.

Rock turns towards the van.

Ace, my man and larry, yo what's up larry?

I heard about the contest. Larry replied.

Yeah! Rock paused.

Get yours dude. Said larry.

As Ace starts down the block. Cool out rock. Ace stated.

Yeah, later on. Rock replied.

Later at home, Rock is in bed holding peables in his arms. Thinking while rubbing peables on the head.

At The Church

People are singing, clapping their hands and praising God. Rock, Ace, Cookie and some of Rock friends from the church are enjoying the service.

With a feeling of stress and anxiety and depression a big sign of relief. Wow man this is wonderful. Shouted Ace.

Yeah, it's nice to show God that we appreciate him. Rock replied.

(Smiling) Nah man, I mean the ladies! The preacher began to announce the altar call

It is now time for the call to worship. All rise, those willing the preacher said.

Yo man, are you going up? Rock look at Ace

Yeah, are you going? Ace look at Rock, puzzled

Who me, (smile) thanks, but no thanks. I still have a few more appointments I have to attend to.

Rock paused before responding. Oh, appointments? Rock looks puzzled

Yeah, there are still a few more girls I haven't laid yet. Rock smiles as he gets up to make his way to the prayer line.

You're crazy. Rock walks up to the prayer line. The preacher begins to pray.

Three hours later church is over and the people are coming out. Cookie comes out of the church and walks up to little rock.

I am going to catch a ride with sister smith okay.

Rock is busy laughing with Ace, didn't hear his sister cookie.

Oh, say what? Rock asked.

I'm going home now, I'm catching a ride with sister smith okay.

Rock still smiling from the joke. Okay. He replied.

Cookie reaches over and gives rock a kiss on the cheek. Rock smiles as cookie leaves.

Well, it's just eight more days now Ace said.

Yup I can hardly wait. This is the chance of a life time Rock replied.

Ace pat's Rock on the shoulder. I'm proud of you homeboy. It's yours for the asking. Come on, lets go home.

Ace places his arm around Rock as they walk towards the car. With a lot on his mind, they crossed the street. Ace pat's Rock on his back twice.

The count down of the contest little rock training like never before that week. Little Rock is sitting down as his hair is being braided, each time one braid is finish he start training on a different routine. Rock doing push ups now then after every two braids he's doing something different like sit ups, then bench pressing, squatting, jogging, in the sand on the beach. When the girl finished braiding his hair, Rock view himself in the mirror with pride and respect.

Rock's House

A week later, the day right before the contest, Marie arrives at Rock's House. The door bell rings. Rock is in his room playing with peables. Then the bell rings again.

Okay peables, take a easy. I am coming. Rock gets up off the bed and walks out of the room to answer the door. The bell rings again as he approaches the door. Rock opens the door. Looking very surprised as he stares at the person standing in his door way.

Well, may I come in Marie asked. Rock looking puzzled

Yeah why not. Marie walks into rock closes the door and they enter the living room. So what brings you here? With a soft sweet voice.

The baby. You see tomorrow I'm expecting and I want my child to have a daddy, not just a father. Marie starts towards Rock slowly. Then she flees into his arm's, while acknowledging her wrong doing. As she talks she breaks down in tears.

I love you little rock, I really do. I am sorry for what happened in the past. At this point, the love that little rock has towards Marie begins to come alive once more.

It's okay, it's alright. Rock wipes the tears from her eye's.

Come on, you have to save your energy for tomorrow. Marie raises her head and Blushes. Rock reaches over and kisses Marie.

Are you okay? He asked.

Marie nods her head. Here, sit down. All of a sudden she feels the baby kick.

Huh, huh.as she places her hand on her stomach.

What's wrong baby? Rock asked.

Oh nothing. It's just the baby playing I guess.

Little Rock, you are coming to the hospital tomorrow right?

I wish I could baby, but tomorrow is the contest.

Gritty her teeth, oh yeah, that's right. So the contest is more important than your child right. Rock gets up

Yeah right! He pause of course not. It's just that tomorrow is the day I've been sweating so hard for to become something and to be successful. Not everybody gets this opportunity. I don't know if you understand me or not. It's not that I don't want to go to the hospital and everything, but it's just that I've been praying for this moment you know, and training hard too.

Little Rock tries to tell Marie how hard he trained and how badly he wished for this moment, but marie wouldn't understand and didn't want to hear anymore of what little rock had to say, Marie stands up Oh, and like I wasn't praying for this moment, well, fuck it then, you enjoy yourself. Blindly in anger, Marie walks toward the front door. All of a sudden the pain returned. Holding her stomach, she braces against the door. Rock reacts quickly.

Oh no. He ran over to her and helped her onto the sofa.

Come on Marie

As he places her on the sofa

Breathe, come on, take a deep breath, that's it, breathe.

Marie began to settle down.

I'm going to call an ambulance. Hang in there baby. Rock rushes into the bedroom to call for an ambulance. He picks up the receiver and dials 911.

Hell, yes, could you please send an ambulance to 1502 Mott avenue.

(Pause)....

Yes

(Pause)...

Little Rock Fortune....

(Pause)....

No this ain't no joke, my girl is getting ready to have a baby,

Yes.

Meanwhile, the pain stopped, temporary. Marie got up and left. She got inside her car and drove away as her eye's began to fill with tears and her heart with love for both little rock and the unborn child she carries.

CHAPTER TWELVE

Switching back and forth between St John Hospital, and Little Rock's House

At the hospital, the nurse is on the phone talking to rock.

Okay, just relax, everything is going to be alright, the ambulance is on it's way. Do you have a watch? The nurse asked.

Yes little rock answered.

Okay, take down the time every time she has a sharp pain. Make sure she is lying down straight. Are you the father of the baby?

Yes little rock answered.

Okay good, her mind should be relaxed. Everything will be okay Mr. Fortune. The ambulance should be there shortly.

Thank you, Rock hangs up the phone and runs back into the living room to marie, but to his surprise she was gone. The sudden impact was too, much for rock to take. He rushes to the door yelling out her name.

Marie!!!!!!! Marie!!!!!!.... But to no avail. Realizing that she shouldn't be driving.

On The Street

Marie speeding down the highway with anger and love dangling in her mind. The pressure begins to build up in her mind, as the tears flow from her eye's and the sweat soaks her body. She starts to get dizzy and could hardly see in front of her. The pain began once more, flowing throughout her entire body. She began to go into labor. The car goes out of control and runs off the road smashing dead into a tree. The front of the vehicle was destroyed. Dark smoke and liquid escape from the wreck vehicle. Someone spotted the vehicle off the side of the road and call 911, Fdny Ems along with highway responded quickly on the scene. They were able to free Marie from the wrecked the smoke was put out they foam the whole car with some type of light brown yellow foam that look like pancake mix in a foam substance. Fdny treated Marie on scene and observed that's she's pregnant. They have a pulse but a weak one and barely a heart beat from the unborn child. They dashed to their vehicle quickly as they could before you know it they we're on the streets with a police escort, by the 101pct the Rmp sirens we're on the patrol car along with the ambulance lights flashing, racing to the hospital.

At the hospital

The nurse consulting with the head doctor. Holding a piece of paper in her hand.

A side from her drivers license, this phone number of a Mr. Little Rock Fortune is the only piece of information she had on her. Should I call this person doctor?

Yes nurse, maybe he is a relative or can get in contact with one. Answered the doctor.

Yes doctor. Replied the nurse. The doctor walks away. The nurse picks up the telephone and dials the number.

Rock's House

Rock is lying on his bed holding peables and thinking about Marie and his child. Then the phone rings. Ring,....ring... Rock picks the receiver up.

Hello Marie, oh I'm sorry. I thought you were somebody else. Yes, this is Mr. Fortune.

(Pause)

My name is nurse Thompson. I'm calling from St. John Hospital here in Far rockaway. A young lady by the name of Marie Johnson was in a vehicle accident. She is...

Stunned by the terrifying news rock cut her off.

What! When?

About an hour ago and

Rock did it again cutting her off.

I'm on my way. Rock hangs up the phone, grabs his coat and runs out the house rushing to the hospital.

At Vanessa's House

Vanessa after entering her house and putting her bag down, takes off her coat and lays it down over the love chair. Then the phone rings. It rings twice before she picks it up.

Hello

Hi vanessa Stephine said

Oh, hi vanessa.

Girl where have you been? I've been trying to reach you.

Oh I went clothes shopping. Girl you should see what I brought from Alexander. Vanessa stated.

Oh, you haven't heard huh! Replied Stephine.

Haven't heard what? Stephine didn't say anything. Vanessa, started wondering and getting bad vibes, and asks Stephine in an atoning tone of voice.

Stephine, I haven't heard what?

About Marie. Stephine begins to cry.

Marie, oh my God!!! Vanessa, finding a chair, sits down.

A few hours ago, she was involved in a serious car accident. Said Stephine.

No!!!! She (pause) No!! Speaking quickly.

How is she? Is she alright? And the baby, what happen to the baby?

Marie is in bad shape, very bad.

she (paused)

and the...

she (paused) again

The baby Died.

Oh God,

(Paused)

Have you called her mother? Asked vanessa.

Yeah she is on her way to the hospital. Marie is at St. John Hospital.

Okay, I am leaving now. Vanessa replied. She hangs the phone up, grab her coat and purse and exits out the door.

At the hospital

Rock walks up to the front desk and ask where he can find Marie. The love that rock has towards Marie is greater than ever.

Excuse me

He takes a deep breath.

Was a young lady by the name of Marie Johnson admitted here this evening.

Just a minute, I'll see. The nurse replied. She looks over her list

Yes, Marie Johnson, they just brought her into the emergency room.

Thank you, Rock takes off running down the hall towards the operating room. The nurse tries to stop him, calling him back.

Wait!!!!

Wait!! A minute you can't go down there. Hey stop him, somebody stop him. Yelled the nurse.

CHAPTER THIRTEEN

On The Streets

Meanwhile Ace is speeding his car down the block headed for Little Rock house. Big-D and Q-tee are also coming up the block. Ace pulls up onto the sidewalk, stops the car and jumps out racing to the front door. He bangs on it. Peables starts barking. Banging continuously, still there was no answer at the door. Big-D and Q-tee see and runs toward the house. Thinking that rock is in some sort of trouble, Q-tee yells out as he and Big-D roll up onto ace.

Hey!! What's going on shouted Q-tee.

As turns around Big-D singed him up against the house.

You better start talking and quick before I fly that head.

I am looking for Little Rock. Ace said.

We kinda figured that, replied Big-D.

No you miss the picture. Rock and I are home boys. The reason I'm trying to find rock is because his girl has been in a car accident.

What!! D yelled

Maybe he's already at the hospital Q-tee said if what he's saying is true. Let's go! They rush inside Ace's car. Ace takes off speeding down the block. Running red lights, breaking all the rules, racing towards the hospital.

I have a good idea which hospital they took her too. Ace stated.

All of sudden, flashing lights were everywhere. Ace stops at the hospital and tells Big-D and Q to go ahead.

You guys go ahead. I have to take my car out for a spin. Big-D and Q-tee gets out of the car and runs into the hospital. Ace takes off fading into the distance with two Rmp police cars chasing him.

At the hospital

Pushing nurses and doctors out of the way, Rock rushes into the operating room. There he saw his Marie lying on the table hooked up to machines. Rock heart was crushed. Tears began to escape from the corners of his eyes. Suddenly the heart machine that kept up with her heart beats stopped. Rock screams out.

No!!!!

No!!!!!!

The doctor's turn around and rush to aid Marie. Big-D and Q-tee arrived in the building of the hospital. Looking for rock, they b Egan running down the hall straight for the operating room.

Meanwhile the doctors are trying to do all they can to get her heart to beat again, but to no avail. But nevertheless they kept on trying. Rock just knew it was all over. He began to get upset, taking the blame and guilt out on himself. Q-tee and Big-D found rock coming out of the emergency room. They rush towards him, they began throwing questions at him to find out what had happened and is she alright.

Hey Rock, how is she man? Q-tee asked

What's wrong? Replied Big-D

But rock didn't say a word, he just stared at them. The doctor came out, Q-tee and Big-D went over to the doctor to find out the results.

Hey doctor!! As he walked towards him. How is she? Q asked.

She's is okay. She just came out of the coma. He replied.

Q-tee and Big-D jump up and slap hands together and said "alright"

Yo Rock, they turn around to tell rock the good news, but he was gone. Where did he go? Q-tee looks at Big-D

I think I know, come on,

Reply Big-D...

They ran toward the door. A man is standing in the way, but Big-D grabs him, Move!! And pushes him out the way as they ran off.

At the bar

Rock went to a bar. There he sat for hours, drinking, then he thought he saw Marie over at the counter ordering a drink. Rock starts to look puzzled as he at the lady near the counter. Then realizing that he is drinking and the effects that are taking place, he doesn't pay the lady anymore attention. Minutes later, two members of the Edgemere projects walks into the bar looking for some fun. They scanned the area and then set eye's on the young lady at the counter. They walked up to her. Their body language we're so amazed to find such a beautiful young lady.

Holy shit!! Hey sticks, check this bitch out!! Bones shouted. Stick turns around.

Wow!! Replied stick.

As he looking her up and down.

How's it going baby, any luck tonight? The crew laughed. The lady looked at stick in the face and said with a nasty attitude.

Suck off!!

As she starts leave the counter before she could take three steps, stick grabs her by the arm and shoves her back up against the bar counter.

Mmmmmmmmmmmmm I don't mine if I do.

He rips her blouse while bones giggles on the side, as he tries to Suck her chest.

Meanwhile rock is watching everything that is going on. And just because the lady resemble Marie somewhat, Rock interferes. He walks up to them, stone drunk.

Leave her alone!!

Stick stops, turns around

Fuck you replied stick. Bones steps in front of sticks.

Hey stick, he is one of those punks that was in the park. Bones said.

Sticks pushes the lady aside and he and bones charge rock. Then they began fighting.

The bartender broke broke the fight up by threaten to call the police if they didn't stop. Rock was hopeless. Stick grabbing bones

Let's go he mumbling.

As they walk towards the door, bone said

You gotta come out side, I'll be waiting for you mother fucker!!!

They walked out the door. The lady helps rock up to the nearest table.

Come on, huh, will somebody please help me!!! Two men help the lady pick rock up to the table. Thank you she replied.

As she placed her hand upon rock's forehead, she began to fall for him and felt sorry for him. Many nice things were going through her mind.

As Rock was coming to she said

Thank you for stepping in.

Yeah I am, huh!! No problem, look I got to go rock replied

Rock knowing that the two gang members are still outside, he tries to get up so he can leave, but she was so concern that she didn't let him leave.

No, please!! You can't go out there now, they're still out there.

I must go now. He stated

Feeling dizzy, he falls into the lady's arm's she placed him back into the chair. Rock feels that today just don't seem to be little rock's day. All of a sudden Big-D and Q-tee arrived. They came busting through the door looking for Little Rock. They spotted him and went running towards him.

Rock, are you alright? Asked Q-tee. The lady shows a sign of relief.

Are you his friends? She asked. The lady explains to Big-D and Q-tee what happen.

Thank God your are here it was terrible, these two big guys came in and started harassing me and your friend here, In a mean tone of voice Little Rock! Big-D replied The lady got even more shaken up Yes, he came over and they beat him.

Sniffing her nose she began to cry.

It's okay were here now. Come on rock, let's go Q tee said. While lifting him up.

You can't go out the front entrance because they're waiting for him to come out the front. She stated. Q-tee looks at Big-D

D slaps his fist into his hand.

Let's go said Q-tee. They left out through the front entrance, Big-D walked out of the bar first then all of a sudden the two gang members came flying into the bar with Big-D right behind them. Q-tee, while holding rock and the lady just got out of the way in time. Q-tee recognized one of the guy's.

That's the guy who stabbed me I'm gonna go talk to him. Here

He passed rock to her.

Take rock to the car.

The lady name is Tina, nervously she takes rock outside. So afraid, she forgot to asked Q-tee where is the car parked or what make or model even what color it is....

While holding rock and searching through the parking lot, Tina whispers to herself

Where is the car? All confused she stops walking as the tears rolling down her cheeks. In a out burst I don't know where the car!!!! I don't know what kind of car it is I don't...

Little Rock is pointing in front of her

It's right there,

He pause

The blue one. The door was open she open the rear door and They both enter the car..

After the fight Come on, lets go said Q-tee. The bartender calls the police. Q-tee and Big-D exit the bar walking towards the car. Big-D walks over to the driver side Q-tee is over at the front passenger side, Big-D opens the door, Q-tee opens the car door on his side and they both got in. D starts the engine, puts the car in reverse and runs over the two gang member's moto pads, Then quickly, he puts the car in drive and takes off racing down the street.

CHAPTER FOURTEEN

At Rock's House

Later arriving at Rock's House, Big-D stops the car.

Thanks fellas rock said.

Don't mentioned it replied Big-D

Just be ready tomorrow. Said Q-tee. They laugh, Rock and the lady Tina gets out of the car.

Listen, take care of him okay?

Tina smiles.

In a soft voice

I will

She said.

Q-tee sticking his head out the car window

Get some rest rock. He shouted.

Then they drove away. As the lady helped rock up the steps of his house. Rock sees a note on the front door from cookie.

Oh by the way what's your name? Rock asked.

Tina she replied

Rock looks up at the door and sees the note.

Oh no, now what?

Rock reaches for the letter as Tina helps him in.

Oh great, my sister mm is out of town just just when I need someone to message my body.

Tina helps rock to the chair in the living room. Looking at Rock with desire.

I'll do it.

Nah, it's okay, you're done too much as it is. Rock said.

Hey, it's no problem.

Tina sat next to rock

I want to

She places her hands on Rock's shoulders rubbing them. As Rock begins to fall asleep, she reaches over and kiss him on the lips and wouldn't stop.

Slowly waking up, realizing what's going on.

I think I'll take a rain check on that rub down okay tina, cause I gotta get up in the morning. Tina stopped kissing rock she gets up

I understand. Thanks for everything. She said.

Walking towards the door. Rock begins to get up.

No, no don't get up, I'll let myself out. Take care little rock.

She opens the door and leaves. Rock gets up slowly, goes over and locks the door and made his way to his bedroom. He opens the door and peables comes running to him.

Peables, what's going on?

Rock picks peables up and kiss her as he glances at Maries picture sitting on his desk. Tears began to flow as he placed peables down. Rock then looks at peables and says

Hold the fort girl, I am turning in.

Peables bark twice as Rock jumped in bed...

Morning The day of the contest

Outta all the morning this year this morning was the most important morning of them all. The sun was out you can smell change in the air. But there is a little wind blowing. it's seem like the world is watching. Feels like everything, birds, homeless people, even the mailman, had their fingers crossed. This was big to the people in this town and the city. This could be the life changing experience for someone if he or she strive harder, believing in themselves, no matter what people say, or no matter the odds in front of you. You can make it....

Rock coming out of his house, runs down the steps towards Q-tee and Big-D who are waiting for him by the car. They open the car door and got in. Big-D put the car in reverse, backs up, turns the car around and skidded down the block speeding to the contest. Flying down the street, Big-D makes a sharp right turn, then a left, a right, an another right and a left. As they approached the theater where the competition is being held, they can see the crowd on line paying to get into the building to see the show. After Big-D parked the car, they started walking through the crowd with Big-D in front pushing the crowd back making way for Q-tee and little rock. Move, get out the way, move Big-D was getting frustrated.

D, be nice, relax D. Q-tee said.

This is bugging me out. They see me coming, why don't they get the hell out my way. Big-D replied.

D, calm down D said Q-tee.

As they continue to make their way through the crowd. In a mean tone of voice.

Little Rock, iam telling you, you better win this shit!

Approaching the door, Big-D is so burnt about making his way through the crowd that he grabs the person who is standing in the door way Q-tee grabs his arm and whispers mole larry the cheese D starts laughing as he walking in the building. They checking bag's if you are competing you have to show your entry form from there you have to go see their doctor.

He have to test you to see if you're takin enhanced drugs if so you can't compete ...you have to be drug's free for six to eight months ... some cases even longer. . After passing all the test, the blood test then the polygraph test Q-tee is helping rock warm up with some poses.

Hmmmm let's a double biceps, Q-tee asked. Rock does a double biceps . Then he began to day dream about Marie while looking in the mirror. Several thoughts and moments of the times they had whether it was on the beach playing in the sand or the sky sky night when they were in the lifeguard chair holding one another glazing at the star's. And when they went to the movies and they kiss for the first time , moments when she had fell asleep when Rock was training and she woke up and just smile he glance back at her then focus on ,training knowing if he win he would make her so proud of him and they both can start a wonderful life together enjoying the finest things in life. Rock was killing the routine Q-tee was very please and impress with what he see in rock.

But still to this point little rock doesn't know if Marie is alive. The only one's who knows is his Manger, Bodyguard ,and Marie's mother.

Hey Q, I think you should tell him. Big-D said

Nah ,D, if I tell him now he'll want to go to the hospital replied Q-tee

Big-D look at Q then he glance at Rock, he looked at Q again

Fuck that ! Look at him Big-D shouted

Big-D waving his finger at Q tee

You better tell him or that's your ass. Q-tee turns towards little rock. Rock begins to come out of the day dream trans as he hear Q-tee calling him.

Little Rock, Little Rock! Q tee shouted.

Rock's mind is back in the room .

Are you alright son?

Huh, oh yeah, I am okay. Rock replied.

Come on, you're on, now remember this is it.

They began to walk towards the door. Big-D opens the door as they walk out

You look good Rock. It's yours, just waiting for you ...

Big-D grabs Q tee before he walks out the door.

Tell him or make a wish!

They stared at each other for a while, then Q-tee nodded his head in a yes decision. Big-D let's Q-tee go

Q tee leaves the room . Big-D paused for a moment and then he leaves behind Q-tee. Q caught up to little rock and calls him by his name

Hey Rock,

Rock turns around

I got to tell you something. You can see it the desire, the determination, the hurt, the pain and the tears in rock's eye's Q tee stop and think about what would happen if he tells rock the truth about Marie. From that thought Q tee changed his mind. He looked at Rock with tears in his eyes. Then he reached over and embrace rock.

Go get it brother!

Thanks for everything he pause

You better go! Replied Q-tee

Yeah you're right.

Rock looks very confident as he walks alone to the stage entrance. He stops at the entrance and waits for his name to be called. Q-tee turns around and heads for the exits door. He opens the door and finds this masses body in his way. Q-tee looks up, it was Big-D. In a firm concern voice.

Did you tell him? He asked.

I started to tell him, but being that I am his friend I'll take the ass kicking.

He (paused).

Well, I would much rather try to take the ass kicking instead of seeing him return back to the streets. To that concrete jungle life style .here he has an opportunity to get out.

Dee looks at Q tee. Stared for awhile, then said.

I am glad you didn't tell him, because Marie is dead. She die a few minutes ago.

Oh shit Q tee replied

Yeah tell me about it Big-D said.

Big-D and Q-tee hung their heads down in sorrow as they walk to the stage viewing booth. Alot of people attended, the turn out was great. The crowd went crazy as the announcer introduced the body builder's. Tina watching over anxiously with her fingers crossed. The music is playing, people is screaming, as the announcer walks up to the microphone.

Okay good evening ladies and gentlemen. We are ready to start the evening, are you ready !!!

The crowd cheers screaming whistling.

Alright.... Now as you all know each of two classes, medium and tall, carries titles, Most muscular, Best poser, and Overall. After the most muscular and best poser titles have been awarded, the body builder's in each class, will all compete in a five place, sweat popping, muscle straining show down for the best overall title. Then as we move on, we come to the highlight of the evening. This will commencement with the winner of the best overall title , in each class. Competing for the title of all titles, a Dennis Magical P&I Association. .. Mr. Muscle Man !!!!!!

The crowd cheering , blowing whistles, screaming as the announcer continued. ..

CHAPTER FIFTEEN

The winner of this prestigious title will have accomplished one of the most spectacular honors in amateur bodybuilding. It will also take him one step closer into the professional field of bodybuilding, along with this honor and other royalties, he will also receive, now get this, a check for 2 Million Dollar's.

The crowd lost their minds of cheers as the music began to play. Alright here they are folks, the night of the future champions.

Cheering from the crowd as the body builder's came up on stage. Rock walked up the steps onto the stage. The camera's panel around him as Tina and the fans began cheering. Q-tee and Big-D looks on with confidence. The bodybuilders are all on the stage facing the audience. Then the competition began. The announcer tells the body builder's to relax. .

Relax Gentlemen.

He pauses, the body builder's start relaxing a little bit .

Gentlemen Double biceps

The bodybuilders show a double biceps pose. Rock looks around first, then he did his

OK gentlemen relax.

They relax.

Gentlemen a third degree turn to the right

They do a third degrees turn.

A side chest pose showing the calve and thigh slightly bent .

Everyone does one.

Okay gentlemen relax.

They all relax.

A quarter turn to your right.

They do a quarter turn.

A back lat spread with one leg kicked back

They do a back lat spread.

Okay gentlemen relax.

They relax.

A back double bicep with one leg of your choice kicked back showing calve

They do it . The crowds reactions was nonstop of ooh, and aaaaa, and a couple of damm!!!

Okay gentlemen relax.

They relax. The crowd is going crazy. Blowing whistles!!!!

Quarter turn to your right .

They all turn to their right.

Side chest pose. Showing calve and thigh slightly bent.

They do it .

And a quarter turn to your right again gentlemen.

They do it .

Your best abs shock pose.

They do it . Some was so intense you can hear the the stomach muscles ripping cracking into place .

Okay gentlemen relax.

They relax.

A left side, side Tricep pose with thigh slightly bent showing calve

They do it .

A right side, side Tricep pose with thigh slightly bent showing calve.

They all do it .

Gentlemen relax, now face the judges, gentlemen if you will please .

They all turn toward the judges

A most muscular pose.

The crowd started cheering as they did the pose. Rock's mind started flashing back on Marie's death.

Relax gentlemen

They relax. Rock wipes his forehead.

Just relax as the judges score as they see it.

Someone shouted from the crowd, "little rock ! You know you got it"
The crowd started cheering.

Okay gentlemen, that's all for now. Come on folks!! Let's hear it as the body builder's walk off staged.

The crowd cheered like crazy. The music stopped. Then a different music came on. The lights were turn off and one by one the bodybuilders came out with their type of music to perform. After the fifth person, Rock was next to come on stage.

The music came on, Q-tee and Tina watching very intensely. Big-D watched nervously while feeding his face. When Rock finished posing, the crowd went so crazy that they gave rock a standing ovation as he walked off the stage.

I'm about to read off the winner of the three major titles replied the announcer.

Most muscular, number sixteen, Little Rock Fortune!!!

The crowd cheers as Rock came out to receive his reward. The lady hands Rock the trophy. Rock reach for it and kisses her at the same. As ro c k started to walk off the stage, the announcer stops him by saying.

Wait a minute little rock, don't go anywhere because the winner of best poser is little rock fortune!!! Tina leaps up screaming with joy as the crowd cheered. The hands Rock the trophy. Rock smiles as he received it from her. Come on, lets hear it folks. They cheer, as Rock walks off the stage. Yeah!!! I love love it, you crazy bunch of

He smile

Hurt my ear people,

He glance towards backstage

Remind me to see my ear doctor.

The crowd laughed. All the bodybuilders returned on stage for the final countdown. They all facing the judges.

Judges, may I have your score cards please.

One judge hands the announcer all the cards.

Okay in 5th place, number 20 Ron filler. The crowd cheered as he steps forward to receive his trophy. In 4th place he pause, number 12 Don Boston he raised his hand as he stepped forward for his trophy. And in 3rd place, lets hear it for Eric Brown. The crowd cheered as he steps forward to receive his trophy. And 2nd place goes to Darryl White. Crowd cheer as he steps forward to receive his trophy. Then the cheering increased. And now he pause. .. 1st place goes to

The crowd yelling out little rock , Little Rock , Little Rock, that's right you guessed it. Little Rock Fortune! !!! The crowd welcome little rock with a standing ovation. As he walks up to receive his trophy, Tina started crying. Q-tee said

It's not over yet!!.

Okay gentlemen, good luck next time hope to see you in the future. You may leave the stage. The rest of the body builder's started walking off the stage.

And now!! The moment we all have been waiting for. Who will be the one to break into the professional ranks of bodybuilding and receive a lump sum check for 2 Million Dollar's to start off. We have two contestants. They are the overall winner's of their class. Their names are Tony Walker and Little Rock Fortune.

The crowd cheering as they return on stage. After going through the four manual poses, the battle began. Okay folk's. You know your favorite, come on, cheer him on !!!!! The announcer turns towards the two bodybuilders, Good luck gentlemen !! They began to pose. The crowd hoes wild !!! Q tee and Big-D look on intensely, Tina is yelling, screaming and cheering rock on. The death of Marie returns back to rock's memories. Rock's mind kept flashing back on Marie.

Okay gentlemen, relax.

Rock kept on posing cause he's still in the trans. The crowd cheering away.

Little Rock, okay that's enough. Rock slowly comes out of it.

Judges, may I have the results please.

They passed the score card to him.

Well folk's, who do you think it is ? The crowd began breaking speaking out. Someone shouted out, little rock!

Another person screaming out let's go Tony! !!! Let's go! !! Tony !!!!

Big-D turns around looking at that person with a mean expression.

Tony Walker! ! Someone else's shouted out. .

The crowd cheers, Tina screams. Q-tee looks at Big-D

He did it !!!

And 1st place go's to Little Rock Fortune, the new Mr. Muscle Man.

The audience, standing on their feet, screaming as the lady hands Rock the overall trophy. Mr. Muscle Man. Rock gives the lady a kiss on the side of her cheek, and shakes the announcer hand as he is handed a check for 2 Million Dollar's. Rock then walks up in front of the microphone. The crowd is breaking.

I am

Rock Blushes as tears began running down his face. A female voice yells out .

I love you little rock !!!

Thank you, I just want to say thank you Big-D for introducing me to Q-tee, my manager. Who stuck by me through thick and thin. Thanks Q! ! And also to the judges who selected me, to be the recipient of this title. Over all these outstanding future bodybuilders. And to my neighbors in my community, who came out to cheer me on and support me I wanna truly thank you from the bottom of my heart. I also want to say never ever give up on your dreams and goals for the greatest dream there is ..... The future! !!!!

The crowd cheers as all the bodybuilders came out and lifted little rock in the air. Rock, holding up his check and his trophy, he whispers as the song I'm so excited by the Clark sisters came on . Are yeah! !! The dream!!!! .

As the theme song plays, little rock makes his way off the stage. Big-D, Q tee and Tina make their way back stage. They meet up with little rock, cameraman and news reporter's. Q-tee hugs rock Big-D, carrying some champagne in his hand, rejoicing as they enter the dressing room. Inside the dressing room, some of the contestants pat rock on the back congratulating him. Rock looks around for Tina. He turns to his left, then he turns to his right, but she was nowhere to be found. Then a female with long hair making her way through the crowd, Tina was able to muscle her way in the dressing room. She sees little rock. A female called out to him.

Little Rock,

He turns around. His mind along with his eyes can't believe what's stareing at him. So surprised, he didn't say a word. Tina said

I'm so excited! !!!

She embrace him. His eyes started closing slowly

Then they found themselves kissing . . .

CPSIA information can be obtained
at www.ICGtesting.com
Printed in the USA
FFHW021604280219
50747931-56149FF